FairyTale

A TRUE STORY

Novelization by Monica Kulling
Screenplay by Ernie Contreras
Story by Albert Ash & Tom McLoughlin
and Ernie Contreras

Random House ⌂ New York

http://www.randomhouse.com/

Library of Congress Catalog Card Number: 97-66662
ISBN: 0-679-88812-8
RL: 4.0

Printed in the United States of America 10 9 8 7 6 5 4 3 2 1

Prologue

London, 1917.

Frances Griffiths and her nurse were watching the play *Peter Pan* at the Duke of York Theatre. Tinkerbell the fairy had just drunk the poisoned medicine meant for Peter Pan. The boy who wouldn't grow up leaned down to hear Tinkerbell's dying words. Then he rose to his feet and came to the edge of the stage.

"Tink says she thinks she could get well again if children believed in fairies," he announced. "Do *you* believe in fairies? Say quick if you believe!"

Peter Pan leaped into the air and flew over the heads of the concerned children.

"Yes! Yes! Yes!" shouted Frances with all her heart.

Peter Pan landed lightly back on stage. "If you believe in fairies, clap your hands!"

Frances was a great believer in fairies. She clapped and clapped until her hands stung. Her nurse looked down at her with disapproval. But Frances didn't notice. Her heart was light for the first time in many months.

Chapter One

Elsie Wright scooped a curled leaf into the stream called Cottingley Beck. On the forest floor beside her stood an elegant table and eight chairs made from twigs and dried flower petals. On the table were eight plates made of eucalyptus leaves and eight acorn cups, which Elsie was filling with water.

"Where are you?" she called softly. "Please come…"

Elsie had never seen the fairies she was inviting to her feast, but she knew her brother, Joseph, had. He had even drawn pictures of them, which he kept in a folder in his bedroom. But Joseph was gone now. Every afternoon during the year since his death, Elsie's mother laid flowers at a headstone that said: JOSEPH WRIGHT, 1905–1916, BELOVED SON

OF ARTHUR AND POLLY. HE SHALL GIVE HIS ANGELS CHARGE OVER THEE.

"Please come," Elsie whispered again.

No one seemed to hear her. The stream twisted through the small ravine, rushing under a fallen tree bridge and over a small waterfall. Elsie's mother thought the beck was a dangerous place. She feared Elsie might trip and fall and get hurt, or even worse. But Elsie thought the beck was the most magical place in all of Yorkshire. A deep sense of peace came over her whenever she was here. It was almost as though Joseph were beside her again.

Elsie looked longingly into the woods. Tomorrow her cousin Frances was coming. Frances's father was missing in the war and her mother was dead. Elsie didn't know if she wanted to share the beck with her cousin. Frances might think fairies were a silly notion. She might even laugh at the fairy doll house Joseph had begun and never finished.

Suddenly, Elsie heard her name ring out through the woods. Her mother was calling her. Quickly but carefully, she packed the table and chairs back into their shoebox and ran home. She raced through the kitchen and partway up the stairs, then stopped and turned around, a bit out of breath. When Mother came back into the house, Elsie said innocently, "Yes?"

"Elsie, where have you been?" asked Mother, sounding exasperated.

"In my room," Elsie said, feeling a little uncomfortable with the lie.

But the mud on Elsie's dress told a different story.

"You know you're not allowed down by the beck," said Mother with a sigh. "How many times have I told you? Go and wait in your room till your father gets back."

In the city of London, a man was being strapped into a straitjacket and tied with a thick rope. Then a cable that was attached to the outside of a tall building was wrapped around his ankles.

"Gently," warned James Collins, his assistant, as the man was lifted to his feet by two policemen and passed through the window.

The man, Harry Houdini, was the most famous escape artist in the world. He was short but athletic in build and powerful in personality.

In the crowd below, Frances and her nurse watched as Houdini was hung upside down above their heads. Wrapped up in the straitjacket, he looked like a giant cocoon. At the same time, Sir Arthur Conan Doyle, the famous creator of Sherlock Holmes, was running up the stairs to get a bird's-eye view. He hoped he wasn't too late. He and his three children—two boys and a girl—entered the room out of breath.

"Sir Arthur, I'm so glad you were able to make it," Collins greeted him. "Mr. Houdini will be delighted. He was very much hoping that you would be able to come."

"Thank you very much," Sir Arthur replied.

Looking at his children, he said, "We wouldn't miss this for the world, would we?"

Outside the window, Houdini was thrashing about like a shark on a fisherman's line. His face was contorted with effort as he struggled to get his right arm over his head.

"Forty seconds!" Collins called out, checking a stopwatch.

Sir Arthur's three children stared wide-eyed as Houdini, with both hands now free, unbuckled the strap that was between his legs. He then pulled the straitjacket over his head and, with a final wrench, tore it off and threw it to the ground.

Below, the crowd erupted in cheers, applauding as Houdini spread his arms wide and then bowed upward from the waist. He was helped back through the window and stood before Sir Arthur.

"Incredible, quite incredible!" marveled Sir

Arthur. "If I hadn't seen it with my own eyes, I wouldn't have believed it."

"Do you believe everything you see?" asked Houdini with a smile. He turned to Sir Arthur's daughter, Jean, and suddenly produced a coin out of thin air.

"A penny for your thoughts," he said, handing Jean the coin.

"It was up your sleeve," Jean said.

Houdini chuckled. "Ladies, gentlemen, be warned," he said, rolling up his sleeves. "Never try to fool children. They expect nothing and, therefore, see everything."

With an air of mystery, the great magician opened his hands to reveal an apple. Even Jean was impressed this time! The guests in the room applauded all over again.

Elsie gave a low curtsy like a ballerina. The imaginary audience was applauding her beautiful Dance of the Fairies. "Thank you, thank you all so much," she said.

Elsie was wearing a pink satin dress unbuttoned at the back and draped loosely over her black mourning dress. She had been dancing around her attic bedroom, which had a high ceiling with exposed beams and rafters. The thing she loved most about her room was the doll house that stood in the corner. It was made of twigs, moss, and dried flowers.

Just then, the trapdoor creaked open.

"Fe, fi, fo, fum," said a deep, gruff voice. "I smell the blood of an Englishman..."

Elsie ran behind the doll house and hid as her father entered the room.

"Be he alive, or be he dead..."

Father stalked toward the doll house, then rose up on his toes and glared down at Elsie. "I'll grind his bones to make my bread!"

Elsie squealed in delight but stayed crouched behind the house.

Then the giant turned back into her father, who said simply, "Hello."

"Hello," Elsie replied.

"That's pretty," Father said, pointing to the bright pink dress.

"Mum says we're not to wear colors!" Elsie said. She was so tired of the rule. Joseph had been gone for a whole year, but the entire family still dressed in black.

"Don't be too hard on your mother, Elsie," said Father. "How was she today?"

"The same," Elsie said sadly.

Elsie's father peered into one of the doll house windows and saw the bits of twigs and moss lying everywhere, as though someone had left in a hurry.

"This needs a little work, don't you think?" he said, gently. "Perhaps your cousin Frances will give you a hand. Would you like to come with me to Bradford tomorrow to pick her up?"

Elsie nodded. "She must be terrified, traveling all the way from Africa by herself."

But Frances wasn't frightened. The train that chugged across the moors was full of wounded men coming home from the war. Frances was trying to get one of them to play cat's cradle with her. When she tapped him on the shoulder, the soldier turned and showed her the full horror of his face, half of which had been burned by fire and was unrecognizable. Frances didn't seem to notice.

"Would you help me with my game, please, sir?" she asked.

The corporal frowned. "What are you doing on this train, little girl?"

"I'm going to visit my cousin," she said, holding out her hands with the string wrapped around them. "Just put your finger through the middle there. It won't hurt, I promise."

"On your holidays, are you?" the corporal asked

as Frances wound the string round his fingers. He wasn't particularly fond of children.

"No. Got you!" Frances said gleefully as she trapped the corporal in her string. "My daddy's a soldier like you. He's in France. His name is Sergeant-Major Griffiths. Perhaps you've met him? Put your finger back down."

Frances yanked her hands apart and the web disappeared. The soldier's finger was released.

"Freed you," she said.

"Thank you," the soldier said, feeling a bit confused. But he couldn't help being charmed by the pretty, matter-of-fact little girl.

"You couldn't have met him now, though," Frances remembered. "He's missing, you see. But when he comes back, he's going to bring me some real French perfume."

The corporal said nothing. He knew that when a soldier was "missing," he often didn't come home— ever. The corporal turned the injured side of his face away from Frances.

"It doesn't look so bad, really," she told him.

He sighed. "I look like a monster."

"I'm afraid of monsters," replied Frances. "I'm not afraid of you."

She held up her string game. "Look, a butterfly."

The corporal's face softened into a smile. Then

he turned away again and stared out the window at the passing countryside.

Elsie and her father ran along the platform in the pouring rain. The train had already left the station. All around her, Elsie saw worn and wounded men greeting their families. Suddenly, she spotted Frances sitting on her luggage, playing a string game with a soldier.

"Frances?" said Elsie, shyly.

"Cousin Elsie!" Frances flew off the trunk and threw herself into Elsie's arms. Elsie was a little startled, but pleased with her younger cousin's warm greeting.

"Elsie, Uncle Arthur, I want you to meet the corporal." Frances turned to introduce her new friend, but the soldier had vanished in the crowd.

Chapter Two

Father was driving his employer's van. Mr. Briggs owned almost everything in Cottingley, and he was always introducing the simple village folk to new inventions like the vacuum cleaner. As the van rattled down Cottingley Road, Frances pulled a flyer she'd found on the train out of her pocket and gave it to Elsie.

"What does it say?" Frances asked as the two of them leaned over the flyer.

"Something about a lecture," Elsie replied. "About angels."

The girls looked at each other, amazed. Then Frances began to tell Elsie all the wonderful things she'd seen in London.

"I saw a man hanging upside-down from a

building," she said excitedly. "He was wrapped up like a mummy, with his arms tied behind his back and everyone watching from below. We thought he would fall on our heads, but he didn't. He escaped in less than a minute! It was incredible!"

"Who was this man?" asked Father from the front seat.

"Houdini," replied Frances. "Harry Houdini."

Father parked the van beside a large tree that stood in front of the Wright house, and the girls ran up the path to the door. "We're back!" Elsie called out as she entered the house.

The moment Frances saw Mother coming out of the kitchen, she ran into her arms.

"Frances! We're so happy to see you," said Mother, a little bowled over by her niece's exuberance. "Where have you been? It's so late."

"Her train was full of soldiers," replied Elsie. "They were all wearing bandages."

"They were nice," Frances added with a quick smile. "But some of them looked like they'd escaped from a pharaoh's tomb."

"Gracious me!" said Mother. "Come into the kitchen and get yourself warm. You're such a big girl now."

"Almost nine," said Frances, proudly.

"Well, that's very grown up, now, isn't it?" said Mother.

Elsie looked on, feeling a twinge of jealousy.

Later, Elsie and Frances had a bath in the kitchen. Mother washed their hair and handed them each a towel warmed by the stove.

"Which room is the bedroom?" asked Frances when they were done.

"Top of the stairs," Elsie replied.

Frances rushed to the staircase. When she reached the landing, she opened the first door she came to and gazed in. Elsie quickly reached in and pulled her out.

"*Those* stairs, Frances," she said, pointing to the ones that led up to the attic.

Frances had found Elsie's brother's room. It was kept exactly the way it had been when Joseph was alive. No one went into it, except Mother when she wanted to be alone.

"How did Joseph die?" Frances asked, wandering around Elsie's attic room and looking at everything in it.

"He had pneumonia," Elsie said. "We both had it."

"Why didn't you die, then?"

"I don't know," replied Elsie, softly.

"Well, I'm glad you didn't," said Frances. "But why does Joseph have a room of his own if he's dead? Do you think he's going to come back?"

"No," Elsie replied. "Mother didn't want anything to be moved. So my dad built me this room up here."

Suddenly, Frances spotted the elaborate little house that Joseph had made.

"What's this?" she said, looking into the back of the house, which was open, and reaching for a twig rocking chair.

"Don't touch it!" said Elsie, frowning.

Frances stepped away, surprised by her cousin's sharp tone.

"What is it?" she asked again.

"A doll house."

"Did your dad make it?" asked Frances.

"No," Elsie said. "Me and Joseph did. Mostly Joseph."

Just then, Mother came into the room through the open trapdoor. "Come along now. That's enough talking, the pair of you," she said. "Into bed, young ladies, or you'll catch cold."

"May I kiss you good night?" Frances asked.

Mother looked startled. She was used to her own daughter's quiet reserve. She hesitated a moment, then held out her arms. Frances flung herself into her aunt's embrace and then hopped into bed.

"God bless," she said, sweetly.

Elsie lay silently in bed. How would she ever get used to sharing her mother with Frances?

The next day Father was at Cottingley Manor, working. He had recently bought a camera, and today he was taking a picture of Mr. Briggs's four large dogs sitting in the front seat of Briggs's Rolls-Royce. Father had finished polishing the car and setting up his camera. Now he was trying to get the dogs to sit still while Briggs looked on.

"Come on, man, come on," said Briggs impatiently.

"You won't thank me if it isn't perfect, Mr. Briggs," Father said, looking through the viewfinder.

"Stay, stay!" Briggs called out as the dogs began to grow restless. "Hurry, man, before they do something on the seat."

Suddenly, Hallam, the butler, opened the front door and two cleaning girls ran out, screaming.

"Excuse me, sir, but I believe Mr. Wright is needed in the drawing room on a matter of some urgency," said Hallam.

The dogs leaped out of the car and began barking loudly.

"Launcelot, Gawain, *heel!*" shouted Briggs. "Heel, boys! Come here!"

Briggs marched down the hallway to the drawing room, followed by Hallam, the two maids, and Father.

"It's a totally simple machine. Any fool can use it," he said angrily. "Why does everybody have to come bleating for Mr. Wright every time it so much as sneezes?"

Inside the drawing room, the vacuum cleaner, which was meant to make life easier, was thrashing around the floor on its own. Briggs grabbed the machine and held it up.

"If you lose control, ladies, you simply switch the thing off. Here is the switch. One way is on and the other way means…"

Father called out to warn Briggs that he'd flicked the wrong switch. But it was too late. Suddenly, the vacuum cleaner spewed out a cloud of dirt and dust all over the room—and all over Briggs.

Father looked away, hiding a smile. Sometimes, he thought, the dream of modernization could turn into a nightmare.

Back at home, Elsie had decided that Frances was the right sort of person to take to the beck. The girls had finished breakfast and were staring in wonder at the thickly wooded glade in front of them. "It's so green," remarked Frances.

"Don't you have a lot of green in Africa?" asked Elsie.

"I don't think so," Frances replied. "Not like this, anyway. What's this place called?"

"Cottingley Beck."

"Race you!" shouted Frances, jumping up. Elsie took off after her. Partway down the path, Frances called over her shoulder, "What's a beck?"

"It's an old word for stream," Elsie said. Then she bumped straight into her cousin, who had suddenly stopped short. At Frances's feet was a perfect circle of red-capped toadstools.

"A fairy ring!" Frances cried.

But Elsie wasn't so sure.

"Look, there's another!" Frances said excitedly. "They appear overnight. It's where fairies dance."

"I know that," Elsie said, insulted.

"*Do* you?" challenged Frances. "So what happens if you stand inside a fairy ring?"

Elsie knew exactly what would happen. Joseph had told her many times.

"They capture you and take you away forever," she replied.

The girls looked at each other and shuddered a

little. Then they began to jump around and shriek with excitement. They both believed in fairies!

"Well, come on, then!" said Frances, rushing down the path. "Let's find them!"

"Frances! Stop!" shouted Elsie.

Frances turned back. "What's the matter?"

"There aren't any fairies here," Elsie said. "They've gone."

"Gone? Gone where?"

"They went away when Joseph died," said Elsie, sadly.

"But those are their rings, Elsie. They have to be here."

And Frances ran off to look for fairies.

Elsie and Frances waded into the beck, carrying their boots and stockings. They hadn't found any fairies yet, and in a way, Elsie was glad.

"I told you we wouldn't find anything," she said in a superior tone.

But Frances was sure that if fairies existed at all—and she felt certain they did—they would naturally live here in beautiful Cottingley Glen.

"Have you tried cake to bring them out?" she asked. Everyone knew how much fairies loved gifts.

"Of course I've tried cake!" Elsie replied indignantly. "Don't you think I would have thought of that?"

How could her cousin, who had lived all her life in Africa, where there were no fairies, know anything about them? But Frances said she had always been interested in fairies and had read everything she could about them. Elsie didn't think you could learn much about real fairies from books.

"I know more about the fairies than anyone else alive!" said Elsie, tossing her head.

"Then let's call them," Frances suggested, forgiving her cousin's harshness. "Do you know the chant?"

Immediately she began the chant, with Elsie cautiously joining her:

"Come out from your fairy bower.
Come upon this golden hour.
Come to us, we beg you, please,
Fairies dancing on the breeze."

In the woods, a bird flapped its wings and flew off. But there was another creature present whom the girls didn't see. It was a tree fairy, who suddenly tumbled through the branches of a tree and, spreading his wings, took flight.

Chapter Three

Monday morning at school, Elsie was doodling at her desk. She was drawing a picture of a tree bent over a stream. In the tree's branches was an elegant fairy. She knew her drawings weren't as good as Joseph's, but she loved to draw anyway.

The teacher, Mrs. Thornton, wrote Frances's name on the board. Then she asked her to come to the front to tell everyone about herself. The classroom of drably dressed children thought Frances was odd in her brightly colored clothing. But Frances didn't seem to care. She walked up with such confidence that Elsie winced. She knew *she* didn't have that kind of courage.

"My name is Frances Griffiths and I'm from Africa," Frances began.

Lucy Walters, the class know-it-all, asked the first question. "If you're from Africa, why do you sound so English?"

"Because I was born in England," Frances replied, without missing a beat. "We moved to Africa when I was little. And anyway, South Africa belongs to England. Lots of people there sound English!"

Lucy Walters's nostrils flared. She was angry that she'd been corrected.

More questions were fired at Frances until finally Mrs. Thornton caught on that the students weren't serious. They were just trying to make the new student uncomfortable. But Frances could take care of herself. Before she sat down she asked, "Any *more* stupid questions?"

At Cottingley Manor, Mr. Briggs and his business associates were admiring the model of Cottingley Mill Father had built. Mr. Briggs flicked a switch and the mill lit up like a Christmas tree.

"Magic, isn't it?" he said. "And everything has been carefully worked out by my Mr. Wright here. Built the model yourself, didn't you, Arthur?"

"Yes, sir," Father said. "It's a plan for the electrification of the mill."

"Gentlemen," Mr. Briggs interrupted, "do you

know what time we have to stop work in the winter months, when demand is at its highest, because no one can see the ends of their fingers in the dark? Electrification will increase our profits overnight!"

"I—I don't know that it's possible to work a longer day, sir," Father said worriedly.

"Not longer days, Arthur! More jobs, more shifts, more work! Everyone in this village will see a whole life of prosperity in front of him, from cradle to grave," said Mr. Briggs proudly. "How old's your eldest, Arthur?"

"Elsie's twelve, sir," Father said.

"Six months and she'll be able to start half-time work at the mill," Mr. Briggs went on. "And she'll be safe in the knowledge that she has a job for life. There's not many who'll be able to say *that* when this war's over."

Father nodded. But silently he wondered if a lifetime spent working in a mill was the best thing for his daughter.

Elsie sat on the tree bridge, dangling her feet in the beck, while Frances waded in the stream with her dress tied round her waist.

"What do you call fairy magic?" Frances shouted to be heard above the rushing water.

"Glamour," Elsie shouted back. She liked talking about fairies with her cousin. It was like having Joseph back. "What's a fairy's favorite thing to do?" she called out.

"Dance," Frances replied quickly. "What's their favorite drink?"

"Honeysuckle dew!"

"What are their clothes made of?"

"Spider's silk," Elsie said. "Don't get your dress wet or Mum'll be furious."

"Look, there are some sort of caves here," said Frances, bending over and peering under the roots of an enormous tree.

"Be careful," Elsie said.

Just as Elsie gave the warning, Frances slipped and fell. Elsie ran along the bridge trying to get to her cousin. But Frances, who had been about to shout for help, was staring in wide-eyed wonder at what she saw swimming toward her. It was a fairy—a beautiful half-girl, half-fish water sprite! It shot up out of the water and hovered for a moment before speeding off.

Elsie scrambled down the bank toward Frances.

"Your dress!" she scolded. "Look at you— you're soaked! They'll be furious when we get back."

"I saw one! I saw one!" Frances shouted excitedly. "Did you see it?"

"See what?" Elsie asked.

"The fairy!"

"No," replied Elsie, mystified. She couldn't believe it. She had never seen a fairy. And now Frances had just seen one and she'd missed it!

That night as both girls lay in the dark trying to sleep, Frances asked Elsie the question that had been on her mind ever since she'd seen the water sprite.

"Elsie, did you see fairies with Joseph?"

"Yes, of course," said Elsie defensively.

But Frances knew by her older cousin's tone that Elsie wasn't telling the truth.

"Then you will see them with me," Frances said simply. She believed now more than ever that fairies were real.

"Promise you won't tell anybody else about the fairies?" asked Elsie.

"Why?" asked Frances.

"Just promise. It has to be our secret," Elsie replied.

Elsie and Frances were walking home from school when they spotted Albert the postman. Frances ran after his bike and called for him to stop.

"Do you have anything for me?" she asked. "I'm

expecting a very important letter from France. From my daddy. For Frances Griffiths—that's me."

Albert started rummaging through his sack, but came up empty. He didn't have anything for Frances.

"Well, can you post this?" Frances asked, handing him the postcard she'd written to her friend back home during recess that morning. "It has to go to Africa."

"To Africa, indeed!" said Albert, looking at the card. "Well, now, you get a stamp for it and I'll personally make sure it gets there."

After supper, while Elsie and Father played a game of chess, Mother opened all the drawers in the kitchen, looking for a stamp.

"I had to write," Frances said. "My friend will think I've drowned otherwise. She told me it rained in England all the time."

"She's not far wrong at that," said Father, pointing at the pawn he wanted Elsie to move.

Mother finally found what she was looking for. She picked up the card, stuck on the stamp, and absentmindedly began reading aloud what Frances had written.

"Dear Dorothy, I am very well. Is it nice and sunny? There has been rain for three days now. I

saw a fairy that lives here, too. She was very pretty..."

Father stopped in mid-move.

"Well now, it's been a while since we've heard about *them*, hasn't it?" he said with a glance at Mother. "Frances, we all want you to have fun while you're here, but no one in this house believes in fairies."

"Elsie believes..." Frances began, looking to her cousin for support. But Elsie avoided Frances's gaze.

"What do they look like?" asked Mother. She seemed to be truly interested.

"Oh, they're all different sorts," replied Frances. She spread two of her fingers apart to indicate the right size. "They're about this big, with pretty wings, except for Mr. Bandylegs."

"Mr. Bandylegs!" Father practically shouted. He couldn't believe the fairies now had names.

Frances scrunched up her face and made an ugly face. "He's a gnome!" she informed everyone.

"So, did *you* see them, Elsie?" Mother asked.

Elsie looked down at the chessboard. She couldn't believe this was happening—after she and Frances had made a promise to keep it all a secret!

"Elsie, tell them about the one in the water," Frances said.

But Elsie remained silent.

"Elsie?" said Frances, begging her cousin's help. "I saw one, I really did, in the water! It was all shining silver and green, like a fish!"

"Easy now," said Father, trying to end the discussion. "Maybe you saw a perch flashing in the sun."

Frances stood up. "I certainly know the difference between a fairy and a fish!" she said angrily, and stormed out of the kitchen.

Later, when the girls were asleep, Mother came into their bedroom and gathered up some books that were scattered on the floor. As she did so, she saw the photograph of Frances's mother, her sister, on the bedside table. Carefully, she picked it up. She could see so much of her sister in her niece. Suddenly, Frances was awake.

"I'm sorry, Aunt Polly," she said. "I didn't mean to upset anyone earlier."

"I know." Mother sighed and put the photograph back on the table.

"Do you miss her, too?" Frances asked.

"Yes, I do," Mother said, nodding. "I miss her very much. More than ever, after seeing you." Then she changed the subject. "So, you believe in fairies, do you, Frances?" she asked.

"Well, I couldn't see them if I didn't," replied Frances. "Like angels."

Mother looked surprised. The night of Frances's arrival, she had found a flyer on the kitchen floor. She had guessed Frances had picked it up on the train. DO ANGELS EXIST? A LECTURE ON THEOSOPHY BY E. L. GARDNER, the flyer had announced.

"Ahh," said Mother, gently. "So now you saw angels down at the beck?"

"No. What I mean is, you can't see angels," said Frances. "You just sort of...feel them...watching you. Like my mother and your Joseph."

Mother was touched and amazed by her niece's wholehearted faith. At the same time, she couldn't help wondering what kind of trouble this faith could lead to.

"When you get older, people won't like it when you tell stories that aren't true," she said.

"But it *is* true," Frances insisted.

"I've been to the beck hundreds of times," Mother said. "Why have *I* never seen them?"

"Grown-ups don't know how to believe," said Frances.

Mother could not reply. She was too moved by the simple truth of her niece's statement.

Chapter Four

At the Hippodrome Theatre in London, Harry Houdini was just finishing his world-famous "Metamorphosis" trick. On the stage, there were two cabinets standing on stilts. Houdini helped a girl climb into one of the cabinets, and then he closed the door. He walked over to the second cabinet and, opening the door, showed the audience that it was empty.

"And now, ladies and gentlemen," he announced in a booming and confident voice, "I will vaporize the atoms that make up the body of this young woman and rematerialize them on the other side of the stage."

The audience held its breath. Everyone had

heard of Houdini's "Metamorphosis" trick—some had even seen him perform it before but still could not believe what they had seen.

Houdini was a master of illusion. What the audience didn't know was that in each cabinet was a mirrored side panel that reflected the opposite wall of the cabinet, making the cabinet look empty. But the crowning secret of the stunt was a second girl, a twin of the first, hiding behind the panel in the second cabinet.

The moment of truth had arrived. With a flourish, Houdini flung open the doors of the first cabinet. It was empty! The audience gasped. A drum roll sounded as Houdini walked across the stage to the second cabinet. With an even greater flourish, he flung wide the doors of the second cabinet. The girl stepped out—transferred bodily, it seemed, across the stage.

"Thank you. Thank you," said Houdini, bowing to tremendous applause. "After the intermission, I will present, for your entertainment only, 'Do the Dead Return?'—an investigation into the false claims of mediums and spiritualists who have tried to deceive the great Houdini. I thank you."

Houdini gave a final bow, the velvet curtains closed, and the intermission music began. The great illusionist rushed backstage to his dressing room, followed by the theater manager and two assistants. As he walked, Houdini tore off his jacket, vest, and shirt and threw them at his assistants, all the while complaining.

"The orchestra came in late again. When I raise my right hand, that's the cue. How many times do I nccd to explain? And where'd they find those girls? Do you know how long I could hold my breath when I was their age? Do you?" An assistant had handed Houdini a towel that he used to wipe his face. "Thank you."

"Four minutes and eleven seconds, that's how long," he went on. "That's a total of two hundred and fifty-one seconds! Thirty-seven is a drop in the bucket compared to that."

The illusionist did not see Sir Arthur Conan Doyle, who was standing outside Houdini's dressing room door. As he rounded the corner, Houdini continued his tirade.

"Any movement, and the whole act is ruined. I ask her to hold her breath a lousy thirty-seven seconds! Can't you find me someone who can hold her breath for a lousy thirty-seven seconds?"

As though to make his point, Houdini voiced his final complaint all in one breath. But when he saw Sir Arthur, he smiled and stretched out a welcoming hand.

"Arthur! Come in, come in. I have a few moments."

Houdini's dressing room was a small one, made even smaller by the clutter of makeup, costumes, and piles of letters, bills, and photographs. There was a small bed in one corner and a chair for visitors in the other.

Quickly, Houdini began to pull on another shirt.

"Please fix yourself a drink," he said to Sir Arthur. "I need to get myself ready for the second half of the show."

"Thank you, no," Sir Arthur said. "I came to invite you to be my guest at Windlesham next weekend. I have invited one or two friends who will, I think, amuse you."

"It would give me great pleasure," Houdini answered, with a smile. "And if you will permit me, I will provide a small entertainment."

"Very good," said Sir Arthur. "Excellent, in fact."

There was a knock at the door.

"Sir, Mr. Collins is waiting for you onstage."

It was time for Houdini to show the audience how easy it was to receive "messages from the dead"—if you knew the tricks of the trade.

"Arthur, will you excuse me?" said Houdini, and with that he left.

On his own in the illusionist's dressing room, Sir Arthur looked more closely at the photographs lining the walls. Many were of Houdini's mother, who had died a few years earlier and whom her son desperately missed. One picture had a memorial card attached, with the words IF GOD IN HIS GREAT-NESS EVER SENT AN ANGEL TO EARTH IN HUMAN FORM, IT WAS MY MOTHER. The card was signed H. HOUDINI.

Sir Arthur wondered whether the stories he'd heard about Houdini trying to communicate with his mother were true. He understood this urge to contact a loved one who had passed on. He had lost his own son the year before, from wounds suffered in the war.

As Sir Arthur stepped out into the London night with a full moon above him, he wondered just how far a person might go in order to speak with someone on the other side of the grave.

The silver glow of that same moon spilled into Elsie and Frances's attic bedroom. Suddenly, for no reason at all, Elsie sat up in bed, wide awake. She looked across to where Frances should have been sleeping but wasn't. Worried, Elsie went to look for her cousin. At the bottom of the trapdoor, she saw a faint light coming from Joseph's room. She found

Frances leafing through the folder marked BECK DRAWINGS.

"Frances, what are you doing?" said Elsie, in a terrified whisper.

"Shh!" Frances said.

Elsie cautiously entered the room and quietly closed the door behind her.

"If Mum knew…" she began, but stopped as she began to look around her.

Elsie hadn't been in Joseph's room since the illness. In the corner she saw Joseph's cricket bat. His books were on the floor and his trumpet was on the desk. A toy soldier stood in front of a tiny twig sentry box. Elsie picked up the box and twirled it in her hand. Suddenly, she was flooded with memories of the brother she adored. It was at times like this that Elsie felt that the terrible pain of missing Joseph might overwhelm her.

"He *did* know the fairies, didn't he?" said Frances, holding up a drawing.

"Better than anyone," Elsie replied. "But the grown-ups told him that he wasn't to talk about fairies anymore. They said it was just imagination."

"I wish she could see them," said Frances, gazing out the window into the night.

"Who?"

"Your mum," replied Frances.

"How can she?" Elsie asked.

"I don't know."

Frances looked longingly at the drawing and then out the window once more. She seemed to be asking an unseen spirit to come to her aid. It was almost as if she was willing the fairy in Joseph's drawing to come to life.

Chapter Five

The next day, Father was in the kitchen, rinsing out a developing tray. He had just finished printing the photographs he'd taken of Mr. Briggs's big dogs. Only one of the pictures was halfway decent. The rest of them showed the dogs in various stages of restlessness.

"Well, I don't think it's sensible," he was saying to Mother.

Mother was getting ready to go into town. She wanted to hear E. L. Gardner's lecture on the existence of angels. "Then let me be foolish," she said, pinning on her hat in front of the mirror.

While Mother prepared to leave and Father tried to talk her out of going, Frances kept interrupting.

She had something important she wanted to ask Father.

"Not now, Frances," Father said. He turned back to Mother. "Be reasonable, Polly," he said.

But Mother was determined to go to the lecture. No amount of persuasion would change her mind.

"Please, Uncle Arthur," Frances interrupted for the tenth time. She tugged at his shirt sleeve.

"*You* be reasonable," Mother said. "What difference does it make to you?" She went out into the hallway to get her coat. Father followed on her heels, with Frances underfoot.

"Uncle Arthur..." she tried again.

"Frances, I am trying to talk to your aunt. Will you just wait a moment?" he said, sharply.

But Frances wasn't intimidated by Father. In fact, that's exactly why Elsie had asked her to do this job. Elsie wanted to borrow her father's camera for something and she knew her younger cousin would not be frightened by Father's temper.

"I'm sorry, Uncle Arthur," Frances said sweetly. "It's just that I wanted to look at your camera."

"Well, you'll have to wait," Father said with as much patience as he could muster.

"Please," Frances begged. She wasn't easily turned aside. "I'll be very careful."

"It's not a toy," Father said. "Now, please, just wait a moment."

He followed Mother to the door. "Polly, you've said it yourself. You'd be better off spending more time with the living."

Mother raised her eyebrows. "Meaning?" she asked.

"You know perfectly well what I mean," Father said. "Your daughter needs you. Instead, you sit around holding on to…"

"You can't even say his name, can you?" Mother said. She opened the door to leave.

"I'll come with you, then," Father offered.

"No, thank you. Stay with the girls. I'm going with Mrs. Burke. She knows what I mean. She knows how it feels."

And with those words, Mother was gone.

While Father and Mother were arguing, Frances had been eyeing the camera lying on the table. She listened to the quarrel for a moment, and then, quick as a blink, she grabbed the camera off the table and ran.

It was late afternoon. Elsie and Frances were on their way to the beck, dressed in heavy coats for the coolness of the day. Elsie was running, with Frances trying to keep up behind her. Frances was carrying the camera.

"Did Father say yes?" asked Elsie, stopping.

"Well, almost." replied Frances, handing the camera to her cousin. "What're we doing?"

"We're going to show them the fairies," said Elsie confidently. She had thought all of this over and decided that there was no other way.

"The fairies will never allow it," said Frances. She was shocked that her cousin could even come up with such an idea—one that would put the special, secret world of the fairies in jeopardy!

"I have a way," said Elsie with a knowing smile.

"We can't betray them," Frances warned. "They could put a curse on us. They trust us…"

"It's for Mum," Elsie said decisively. She continued down the path into the glade, with Frances following close behind.

Elsie and her father stood in the darkroom with only the red lamp for light as Frances waited outside. While she waited, Frances watched a fly crawl across the kitchen table. She marveled at the insect. At such close range, it looked like a monster.

In the darkroom, Father had set out the developing trays and was taking down one of the exposed negatives from the shelf by the door. The darkroom was a tiny room under the stairs. Elsie stood at Father's elbow to watch as he submerged the first glass plate into the chemical solution. Father wasn't pleased at the way Elsie had gone about getting his camera to take a picture of her cousin.

"It's just that if you had waited, I could have helped," he said. "A camera isn't a toy, you know. You didn't take a tripod or anything with you, so it'll likely just be a blur. You probably won't see your cousin at all."

"We wanted it to be a surprise," Elsie said. She was up on her toes, anxiously awaiting a first glimpse of the picture.

"Well, next time, *ask*. Do you understand?"

Father lifted the glass plate out of the tray and stared closely at the emerging image. There was a clear outline of Frances sitting in the glade, but flying all around her was what appeared to be twists of wastepaper.

"Well, there's something, but look at all this mess," said Father, peering closely at the plate. "Why didn't you tidy up before you took it?"

Elsie stared at the plate, her eyes wide in shock and delight. That was no mess of paper flying around Frances—those were *the fairies*! "They're on it! They're really there, Frances!" Elsie shouted through the door. "On the plate! I can see them!"

On the other side of the door, bored now with all the waiting, Frances suddenly came to life. "Yes! Yes! Yes!" she cried, dancing wildly in the hall.

Father was staring closely at the image, which hadn't completely emerged. "What's the matter with you two?" he asked and asked. "Have you gone crazy?"

Then he looked back at the plate. There, as clear as day, he saw fairylike creatures flying all around Frances as she sat in the glade.

"What in the...?" Father was too astounded to finish his sentence.

Mother sat in the audience at E. L. Gardner's lecture on angels, fascinated. Gardner, who considered himself a scientist, believed in the existence of angels. He also believed in spirits, unseen by human eyes but influential in their lives.

"All things are possessed of a guiding spirit," he told the audience. "Humans have angels. There are also other, lower, levels of energy, such as salamanders, the spirits of fire, and undines, the spirits of water. Next are gnomes and elves, which are the spirits of the earth and the forests. Finally, there are the fairies, the most famous of all: the spirits of the air."

Mother glanced around. The audience was a

mixed crowd, both in appearance and in their willingness to believe. Many were workers from the nearby mills, mainly women. There were one or two individuals who stood out, such as the well-dressed woman and her awkward husband, who clearly didn't want to be there, and a crippled soldier named Sergeant Farmer.

"Ask any child," Gardner continued. "Ask them who it is that tends our gardens. They'll answer, quite correctly...*fairies*."

Some of the members of the audience began to chuckle or murmur their disbelief. An angry-looking man got up and walked out, muttering to himself about "loonies." Meanwhile John Ferret, a newspaper reporter, scribbled notes on his writing pad. He thought the whole spirit business was a pile of nonsense from start to finish. He stood up to ask a pointed question.

"Er, excuse me, Mr. Gardner," he said with a sly smile. "I'm John Ferret and I'm with *The Bradford Argus*. Have you ever seen an angel yourself?"

"No, and I'm not..." Gardner began.

"Or a fairy?" interrupted Ferret.

"Sir, I am not claiming to..." Gardner tried again.

It was just as Ferret suspected. This man Gardner was a humbug, full of ideas but with no evidence or experience to back them up. "Apologies for the interruption," Ferret said, snapping his notepad closed. "But the paper goes to bed in half an hour—and so do I."

"Sergeant Farmer!" Gardner called out to the crippled soldier in the audience. The sergeant had an amazing story to tell, and if Gardner couldn't save the evening's lecture fast, Ferret would denounce him as a crackpot in tomorrow's paper.

"Would you come forward, please, sergeant?"

With the help of a crutch, Sergeant Farmer walked slowly to the front of the room. He did not climb up on the stage, but stood before the audience and told them of his fateful experience on the night of August 28, 1914.

"My battalion was in retreat from the town of Mons, in Belgium. The German cavalry was about to make a charge and our position was very bad. We had no cover and no prospect of reaching a safe place."

Sergeant Farmer cleared his throat and then continued with emotion.

"So we were ordered to stand and prepare to fight—to die, most likely. As we were waiting, an officer came and took us a few yards away to show us the sky. When the moon came out from behind the clouds, I saw three shapes—all with outspread wings. They were hovering above the German line, facing us. All of the men with me saw them. The men from other groups came up and told us they had seen the same thing."

Mother listened to Sergeant Farmer with every cell of her being. Some of the skeptics among the audience were also attentive. Only Ferret shrugged his shoulders and left the room.

"The enemy saw the angels as well," Farmer continued. "They started to retreat in fear and disorder, and we were able to move to safety. I shall never forget what I saw that night. I have not the slightest doubt that we saw three angels." He paused. "Besides, I should be very sorry to make a fool of myself by telling a story merely to please anyone. I speak the truth." With that, he returned to his seat.

When the lecture was over, Gardner stood at the door, handing out pamphlets. Mother stopped to ask the question that had been on her mind all evening. It was the reason she had come to hear Gardner speak in the first place.

"Do you really think it's possible to see them?"

Gardner noted Mother's black mourning dress and her sad expression.

"Do you mean those who have passed on?" he asked, gently.

"No, I mean..." Mother was suddenly embar-rassed. "I mean...angels or...*fairies*."

"Madam, theosophy is not a religion, it is a sci-ence," Gardner replied. "Of course it's possible—although, I'm afraid, not easy."

Mother was troubled by Gardner's words. When the bus dropped her off in Cottingley Village, she took her time getting home. She needed to think.

Chapter Six

Father had printed the glass plates over and over again, trying to figure out just how the girls had made their photographs. A row of photos lay on the kitchen table. One photo clearly showed Frances, sitting in front of a band of dancing fairies.

Father stared at the photo. "That's another fairy?" he asked skeptically, pointing.

"Oh, no. That's Mr. Bandylegs," said Frances matter of factly.

"The gnome, right?" said Father dryly. He was certain the photographs had been faked. He just couldn't tell how.

"All right," he said finally. "The game's over. How did you girls do it?"

"Do what, Uncle Arthur?" said Frances innocently.

"Elsie?" Father asked, turning to his daughter.

Elsie locked eyes with Frances. How could they get out of this without telling the truth? "We just took the photos, Dad," she said. "They're for Mum."

Father looked from one girl to the other, then shook his head.

"Oh, no, they're not," he said. "She'll never set eyes on them. I guarantee you that. This kitchen will be clean when she gets home, and these photographs will be gone."

A short time later, Elsie and Frances were wide awake, waiting for Mother to return home. Soon they heard the front door open and shut. Then came the sound of footsteps, and then sobbing. The girls tiptoed to the landing and looked down to see Father holding Mother. She was sobbing as though her heart would break.

"What's the matter?" he asked. "What's happened?"

"Nothing," Mother said. Her tears seemed to stop as suddenly as they'd started. "I'm just very tired."

She hung up her coat and hat and started toward the kitchen. But Father stepped in front of her before she could go through the door.

"Don't go in there," he said. "I have to tidy up. You go to bed."

Mother looked at Father suspiciously. She marched past him into the kitchen, where she saw the table covered in papers, magnifying glasses, and photographs.

"What have you got here?" she asked, frowning.

"Nothing," said Father, as casually as he could.

Mother picked up first one and then another of the photographs, looking closely at each. "Did you do this?" she asked.

"No," Father replied. "The girls took them. Look, they were just..."

But Mother was already running upstairs, clutching the photographs in her hand. When she entered the girls' attic room, Elsie and Frances pretended to be awakened from sleep. They rubbed their eyes and yawned.

Mother held up the photos. "They're real, aren't they?" she said excitedly.

The girls looked at each other. Then they nodded yes.

Gardner was rushing to catch the Bradford train at the same time that Mother was rushing to catch him.

"Mr. Gardner!" she called.

Gardner glanced back but didn't slow his pace as Mother ran toward him.

"Forgive me, madam," he said as she came up, breathless. He was somewhat out of wind himself. "My train..."

"I was at your lecture," Mother said.

The conductor leaned out of a window and blew his whistle. The train spit steam and slowly began to move. Gardner quickly stepped up to his carriage.

"Perhaps when I'm in Bradford again..." he said, anxious to take his seat.

"Please have a look at these," Mother said, thrusting an envelope into Gardner's hand. "I must know what you think!"

Gardner just nodded and took the package. The train was gathering speed.

When Gardner was settled in his compartment, he opened the envelope and took out two photographs. He was stunned by what he saw.

"Good heavens!" he exclaimed.

The other passengers in his compartment looked annoyed at his outburst, but Gardner paid them no mind. It was true, just as he had always believed—*fairies were real!* And these photographs proved it!

* * *

Father's camera lay in pieces on the kitchen table. As Father wiped the lens, he told Mother a story about meeting a man who'd come back from the war in France. The man had told Father that if he'd only had a camera with him, there would never be another war. If people could see what he'd seen, the man said, they'd never again be talked into fighting.

"Why didn't he, then?" Mother asked. "Take a camera, I mean."

"He said there were plenty of cameras," Father replied. "But they were always pointed in the wrong direction." He paused and then mentioned what had been on his mind for months.

"Do you ever think about us not having a photograph of Joseph? We have only that one they took at school when he was six."

"I don't need photographs," Mother said.

"Don't you?" Father sighed. "I do. I think of Joseph sometimes, here in this house or out on the street, and...I can't see him. I can't see his face. It changes shape and becomes anybody's face. I can't hold it in my mind. It frightens me. I think that's why I bought this."

Father turned the camera over in his hands.

"Do you think the girls' photographs could be real?" asked Mother, changing the subject.

"No, Polly, I don't," Father said. "I know they can't be." Then he paused and asked more gently this time, "Do *you?*"

"I don't know," Mother replied. "I just don't know. I'm not sure what frightens me more—that the children are lying to us, or that they're telling the truth."

Gardner had taken the photographs of Frances and the fairies to Mr. Harold Snelling, an expert in photographic trickery. Snelling had examined the photographs under a magnifying glass and was now examining the glass plate negatives. Gardner waited impatiently for the verdict.

"Well...?" he asked. "Mr. Snelling, please!"

"Extraordinary, quite extraordinary," Snelling muttered, lost in his examination of the second photograph. "This is the most extraordinary thing I've ever seen. Amateurs. Whoever took these certainly didn't know the first thing about photography."

"They're fake, then?" asked Gardner, disappointed.

"Photographic fakery is an art, Mr. Gardner,"

Snelling told him. "Not something that the amateur could attempt. No, what you have here are untouched, open-air, single-exposure shots."

"And the fairies?" asked Gardner hopefully.

"Personally, I don't know fairies from fireflies," Snelling said. "But there is one thing I can tell you. Look, here at the wings."

Gardner gazed through the magnifying glass and examined the photograph.

"I'm quite certain of this," Snelling continued. "At the time of exposure, *those wings were moving.*"

"The photographs are genuine, then?" asked Gardner, ready to burst.

"As the King's beard" was Snelling's reply.

"If you'll excuse me," said Gardner. Then he grabbed his hat and raced for the door.

Elsie lit the thick candle that was set on the floor between her and Frances. The girls were in their nightdresses, but it was a solemn occasion nonetheless. Their faces glowed with the yellow light thrown by the candle.

"What are we going to do?" asked Frances nervously.

"We're going to make a promise," Elsie told her.

"Are we?" Frances said. "What kind?"

"The kind that lasts forever. Now, hold out your thumb."

Elsie tilted the candle over Frances's thumb and poured off a small drop of hot wax. Frances winced a little from the prick of pain. Then Elsie poured a drop of wax on her own thumb and pressed it against Frances's.

"This is so exciting!" Frances said.

"Shhhh," cautioned Elsie, closing her eyes. "Quiet! Repeat after me: I, Elsie Wright..."

"I, Elsie Wright," said Frances, smiling at her own joke.

"Be serious," Elsie scolded.

"Sorry," Frances said meekly, beginning again. "I, Frances Griffiths..."

"Hereby on this day swear never again to break the code of fairy secrecy," Elsie continued. She frowned at her cousin. "Say it."

"... swear never to break the code of fairy secrecy," Frances repeated, rather reluctantly.

The girls parted their thumbs. Then Frances thought it would be fun to pretend they were at a seance. She waved her hands over the candle, imitating a medium.

"Spirits of the dead," she intoned in her spookiest voice. "We call to youuuuuuu..."

Suddenly, without warning, the candle blew out.

The girls screamed and jumped headfirst into their beds, giggling with goosebump terror. After a moment, Frances whispered, "What happens if we break our promise?"

"We won't," replied Elsie, certain *she* never would.

Chapter Seven

At Sir Arthur Conan Doyle's stately home, twelve guests had just finished their dinner and were preparing to view a demonstration by Harry Houdini. Among Sir Arthur's guests were Geoffrey Hodson, a clairvoyant, and E. L. Gardner, the theosophist. Houdini was standing at one end of the table in front of the double doors. His assistant was setting up a blackboard as Sir Arthur entered, carrying a folded piece of paper.

"Have you written a message as I instructed?" asked Houdini.

"I have," Sir Arthur assured him.

"Please allow me to give it to someone for safekeeping," said Houdini. He handed the note to Geoffrey Hodson.

"Now, Sir Arthur, please choose a piece of chalk from this bowl," Houdini went on.

He held out a small bowl, which contained three sticks of chalk. Sir Arthur picked one, and Houdini handed the chalk to another guest.

"Freely selected, as you see," Houdini said. Then he instructed the man who held the piece of chalk, "Break it open, please, and show it to the table."

The chalk was broken in two and the pieces were passed around. Everyone at the table could now be certain that it was an ordinary piece of chalk.

"Gentlemen, ladies, a piece of chalk, no more, no less," Houdini said. "Now, Sir Arthur, take another."

Sir Arthur chose another piece of chalk.

"Thank you," said Houdini. "Now I must ask each of you to empty your mind of any extraneous thoughts and concentrate on the board in front of you."

Houdini walked around the board, accepted the piece of chalk from Sir Arthur, and placed it on the blackboard. There it stuck, ready to write—all on its own!

Sir Arthur's guests were in awe. There was an electricity in the room that one could practically reach out and touch. And, even more amazing, a sudden cold draft made the candles on the table flutter.

"It feels cold," Gardner said nervously.

"A spirit is present," Hodson informed him, his face paling slightly.

"Concentrate, please, ladies and gentlemen," Houdini said. "I must ask you to remain silent from this point on."

Slowly, the chalk began to move across the board without the help of a human hand, leaving a trail of letters behind it. Houdini was in deep concentration, a hand to his brow. When the chalk was finished writing, Houdini asked Hodson to read the note Sir Arthur had written in the other room.

"Their time will come."

"Are those your words, Sir Arthur?" Houdini asked.

"Exactly as I wrote them!" said Sir Arthur.

With a flourish, Houdini swept his hand toward the board. There, for everyone in the room to see, was the exact same message!

Everyone applauded.

"Thank you," said Houdini, bowing slightly. "But let me assure you all that I was not assisted in this endeavor by any spirit. It is a trick, ladies and gentlemen—but, I hope, a very good one."

There was nervous laughter around the table, and then polite applause, for no one knew exactly what to believe.

Gardner was the first to break the silence in the room. "So you do not believe in any form of communication with the spirit world?"

"I didn't say that," Houdini replied. "It is not my wish to offend anyone's belief. I can only speak of what I have seen with my own eyes. In all my investigations I have yet to encounter the real thing. These people who claim to contact spirits are more interested in raising your money than your dead relations."

"So then, Mr. Houdini, you believe all seances are faked?" asked Hodson, the clairvoyant.

"No, sir, only the successful ones!" was Houdini's quick reply.

Gardner walked around the blackboard, trying to figure out how the trick had been performed.

"May I examine the chalk?" he asked. When Houdini nodded, Gardner bit into the piece. It was exactly what it appeared to be—chalk and nothing else.

"I don't understand," said Gardner, mystified.

"Sir Arthur, how would your creation—the famous detective Sherlock Holmes—explain this trick?" Houdini asked.

There was a murmur around the table. All of Sir Arthur's guests thought the suggestion was a clever one.

"He would not attempt it," said Sir Arthur. "Genius requires no explanation. However—may I look at my note?"

When the paper was handed to him, Sir Arthur agreed that the note was the one he had written. Then he examined the chalk and walked around the board.

"Geoffrey, do you still feel the cold?" he asked.

"No, I don't," Hodson replied. "But I *did*. We all did." The others at the table nodded.

Sir Arthur began to explain Houdini's mind-reading stunt. James Collins, Houdini's assistant, was on the other side of the window and had opened it when everyone was studying the chalk. He'd reached through the window with a magnetic pool cue. Collins had used the cue, along with a piece of magnetic chalk Houdini had substituted for the first piece. That way, it looked as if the chalk was being held on the board by an invisible hand. Collins knew what the message said, since Houdini had substituted a blank note and given it to him while passing the real note to Hodson.

"Am I right?" Sir Arthur asked when he had finished.

Houdini gave Sir Arthur a slight bow, in recognition of his superior sleuthing abilities.

"I first saw this trick performed by the Fox sisters in America," Houdini explained. "But I'm sure that there is no medium anywhere that could withstand so great a detective."

"Do not confuse the medium with the magician," Sir Arthur warned. "Your performance was a demonstration of logic and can therefore be logically explained, but there remains the inexplicable."

"In my experience, the inexplicable can usually be explained," Houdini said.

"Gentlemen, ladies, will you excuse Mr. Houdini and me for a moment?" Sir Arthur asked his guests. He had something he wanted to show the great illusionist.

In the billiard room, lying on one of the tables, were two photographs Gardner had given to Sir Arthur earlier that evening. Houdini glanced at the photos, then tossed them back onto the table.

"Those fairies aren't real," he said, unimpressed.

"These pictures were taken by two children who have never before used a camera," Sir Arthur told him.

"Anything can be faked," Houdini responded with a shrug.

"By two little girls?"

"By anyone."

"May I show you another photograph?" Sir Arthur asked. He picked up the framed photograph that was set on his desk and showed it to Houdini. It was a picture of a handsome young man in a military uniform.

"Your son?" Houdini asked.

Sir Arthur nodded. "He died in London last year after being wounded at the Somme."

"I'm very sorry."

"Two months ago, with the help of Mrs. Annie Brittain, a medium in London, I made contact with him," Sir Arthur continued. "He actually spoke to me. Have you any idea what that meant to me? Do you think I am such an old fool that I could be tricked into believing that I was speaking to my own child?"

"You wouldn't be the first," Houdini told him gently.

Sir Arthur pulled out a bundle of drawings from his desk and showed them to Houdini. They were doodles and sketches of fairies that Sir Arthur's father had made while a patient in the Royal Lunatic Asylum in Edinburgh.

"This is what my father saw," Sir Arthur said. "Every day of his life. He wrote about them, talked about them. They devoured him. You don't have

Frances and Elsie discover a fairy ring.

Frances is the first to see a fairy at the beck.

Father develops the girls' photographs.

Mother rushes to deliver the photographs to Mr. Gardner.

The girls vow never to break
the fairy code of secrecy again.

Elsie and
Frances
search for
more
fairies.

The girls bring the fairies a special gift.

Hordes of people hunt for fairies in the glen.

The postman delivers a long-awaited package to Frances.

The girls and Mother travel to London.

Elsie and Harry Houdini discuss the importance of secrets.

Ferret the reporter snoops for the truth—

—and makes an unexpected discovery!

Elsie thanks the fairies
for their help in bringing
her family together again.

children, Harry, but talk to mine. Ask Jean whether she believes in fairies. She'll tell you she saw one in the very garden not ten yards from where we are now sitting. Elsie Wright's photographs have been pronounced genuine—not by a theosophist or a medium, but by an expert in photographic trickery. I intend to use them in an article I'm writing for *The Strand* magazine."

"People will laugh at you," Houdini said. "You need proof—backup—if you intend to stand up and tell the world you believe in fairies."

Sir Arthur sighed. Then he sat down at his desk, took out a piece of paper, and began to write a very important letter:

Dear Mr. Wright,
My friend Mr. E. L. Gardner was pleased to show me the fairy photographs taken by your daughter and niece. As I shall be staying in the area with friends, I would be very grateful to you if I were allowed to have half an hour's chat with the girls...

Chapter Eight

Mother had cleaned the entire house in anticipation of Sir Arthur Conan Doyle's visit. Trays were laid out on the table with the family's best teacups and saucers lined up. Everything was in tip-top shape. It looked as if the king himself was about to pay a visit.

Mother and Father were dressed in their Sunday best. They seemed very excited, but Elsie and Frances were nervous. After all, they had made a vow never, *never* to betray the fairies again.

"I'm going to be sick," Elsie whispered as Frances adjusted the buttons at the back of her best dress.

"No, you're not," Frances said.

"I am," replied Elsie with certainty. "I always know."

Just then, Father appeared at the trapdoor.

"Elsie, Frances," he said gently. "If there's anything you want to say to me, anything at all, it's not too late…"

He hoped the girls would confess that the photographs were all a hoax before they went downstairs and pretended to a room full of important men that they knew where the fairies lived. He wanted all of them to be spared the humiliation.

"We're nearly ready, Uncle Arthur," said Frances, as though this was what he wanted to know.

"Elsie?" asked Father.

"We'll be down in a minute," Elsie said, avoiding Father's eyes.

Father looked solemnly at both girls. Then he went back downstairs.

When the three grand-looking cars drove up to the small Wright house, it was raining hard. Knowing how much fairies hated rain, the girls had prayed for stormy weather—and here it was!

Sir Arthur had brought along a few friends who were also interested in the supernatural: Harry

Houdini and E. L. Gardner, of course, as well as a Cambridge physicist and two well-known clairvoyants. The six men entered the small house in a flurry of wet umbrellas and raincoats.

Soon the parlor was crammed with men sitting in chairs, drinking tea and eating biscuits. At the girls' entrance, Sir Arthur Conan Doyle stood and the other guests did the same. Elsie and Frances felt as if they were in a forest of giants.

"Frances, Elsie, this is Sir Arthur Conan Doyle," said Mother.

"How do you do?" Sir Arthur said, bending to shake the hand of each girl. "What a great pleasure to meet you both. If I may, I'd like to introduce the members of my party.

"This is Cambridge physicist Sir Oliver Lodge," Sir Arthur began. "And these are the noted clairvoyants Claude Passat and Geoffrey Hodson, and, of course, the eminent theosophist E. L. Gardner. And from America, the genius of escape, Mr. Harry Houdini."

Sir Arthur turned to introduce Houdini, but the genius of escape had escaped.

"Oh, dear," Sir Arthur said. "Well, I am sure he will reappear. May we be seated?"

All of the guests sat down once more, while

Elsie and Frances stood in the center of the room.

"Mr. Gardner had your photographs of the fairies tested," Mother began.

"Merely as a precaution, of course," Gardner said quickly, noticing the girls' frightened expressions.

Mother reached for the photos and smiled as she took them in her hands.

"Oh, they're quite real," Gardner added. "And they are quite extraordinary."

Elsie's knees began to shake. Frances leaned over to steady her older cousin. Then Gardner held out two neatly wrapped packages. "We've brought something for you," he said.

"There's one for each of you," added Sir Arthur.

Elsie and Frances unwrapped the packages. In each one was a brand-new camera.

"How does it work?" Elsie asked, lifting her camera out of the box.

"The same as your other camera," Gardner replied. "I made certain of it."

The girls looked at each other, suddenly very worried.

"Sir Arthur wants you to take some more photographs for him," Mother said.

Elsie didn't know what to say. But without a

moment of hesitation, Frances spoke up.

"Of course," she said confidently.

Elsie glared at her cousin, who seemed incapable of keeping a secret. She grabbed Frances by the arm and pulled her toward the door.

"It'll just take us a moment to change," she called over her shoulder to the others.

Once they were headed up the stairs and out of earshot, Elsie turned on Frances.

"Are you crazy?" she said angrily.

"What was I supposed to say?" Frances replied.

Elsie threw up her hands. "We made a promise." Then she paused, frowning. "Listen," she said.

"What?" Frances asked.

"The rain's stopped."

Now there was no getting out of it. They would have to go fairy hunting. Even worse, now they could only hope that they would be able to come up with another photograph.

"I think *I'm* going to be sick," said Frances.

Houdini had disappeared to explore the house and find out for himself exactly how the girls' photos had been made. When he came upon Father's darkroom, however, he was disappointed to find only those things one would normally find in a darkroom: trays and bottles of chemicals.

Suddenly, Father came up behind him. "May I help you?" he asked.

Houdini turned to offer his hand. "Harry Houdini. I'm sorry, Mr. Wright, but I'm interested in photography myself. I was just curious. This is...where?"

"Where I do my exposures," Father finished. "I use natural light, as you see." He pointed to a tiny window. "And this is where I developed Elsie's pictures, if that's what you're asking."

"I see."

"Mr. Houdini," Father continued, "I don't know exactly what the girls did, but I do know two things. First, there was no trickery in this darkroom. And second, there are no fairies at the bottom of my garden."

While Houdini talked to Father, Sir Arthur found Mother in the kitchen, making tea. He offered to fill the kettle, and while he was doing so he told her about his son. Sir Arthur understood the pain Mother was going through, since he was experiencing the same pain.

"There are no words to describe the loss of a child," Sir Arthur said comfortingly. "But your daughter's achievement must be a great comfort to you."

Mother burst into tears. "I'm sorry. This is stupid of me," she said finally.

"Not at all," replied Sir Arthur.

"May I ask you something?"

"Of course you may," Sir Arthur said.

"Do you believe the girls?" Mother asked. "Do you think the pictures are real?"

"Mrs. Wright, you are the mother of the girl," Sir Arthur said. "And as her mother, you must know a truth that the rest of us can only fumble for. Do *you* believe they're real?"

"Yes," said Mother softly. "With all my heart."

Gardner was carrying the cameras as he trailed the girls down the grassy slope to the beck. He stumbled, then stopped to catch his breath. He couldn't help being struck by the exquisite beauty he saw all around him. He was so lost in admiration of nature that he came back to reality only when he heard Elsie shout, "Look out, Mr. Gardner!"

He had nearly stepped inside a fairy ring!

"Oh, thank you. Thank you, dear girl," said Gardner, very grateful.

"Never, *ever* step inside a fairy ring," admonished Elsie.

"Quite true," Gardner agreed. "I was foolish. Not paying attention."

"You could've been captured," Frances informed him. "Do you know what to do when you're captured?"

"Well, er, I suppose…" Gardner began, not having a clue.

"Don't eat!" said Frances earnestly. "If you eat their food, you can never get back! You'll be trapped forever!"

"We should leave now," Elsie said nervously, looking around. She didn't want the fairies to think she had betrayed them again by bringing a stranger to their home.

"Oh, no, please!" Gardner begged. "I'll be more careful! I give you my word."

Frances took the cameras and told Gardner to stay hidden behind the tree while she and Elsie went searching. Gardner waited anxiously for the extraordinary moment when he would see his first fairy. Suddenly, Father came up, looking for the girls.

"Mr. Gardner, what are you doing?" he asked. "Where are the children?"

"Shh!" Gardner said, with a finger to his lips. "We should keep our voices down. The girls will be herding the fairies back this way."

Father sighed and put his head in his hands.

"I'm certain both girls are clairvoyants—and perhaps mediums as well," Gardner added.

"Together they create an etheric field which allows the fairies to metabolize subtle amounts of ecto-plasm into their bodies. That's how the girls were able to capture them on film."

Gardner stopped when he saw the look of dis-belief on Father's face. "I don't expect you to under-stand," he added quickly.

By now, Father had had all he could take. "Elsie! Frances! Come here!" he shouted down into the beck.

"Mr. Wright, we mustn't interfere," Gardner warned.

"Mr. Gardner, the girls took a couple of pho-tographs in the beck," Father said impatiently. "How they did it, I don't know. But I guarantee you this: it won't happen again."

Suddenly, Frances came running up the slope with Elsie behind her. "Mr. Gardner! Mr. Gardner!" she called excitedly. "We've got them!"

She handed Gardner her camera while Father stood with his mouth hanging open and a look of total confusion on his face.

Chapter Nine

Sir Arthur and Gardner had taken the latest fairy photographs to London to be tested by the experts at the Kodak Company. Now they were following the chief technician, Henry West, through the print room.

"So you have examined all five photographs?" Sir Arthur asked eagerly.

"We have, Sir Arthur," West replied. "The two original pictures and the three new ones that were taken with the cameras you gave the girls. Mr. Binley will inform you of our conclusions."

Two lab technicians carrying a large blow-up crossed their path. It was a blow-up of the photo Gardner called "The Fairy Bower."

"Incredible," Gardner said. "A fairy bower! I questioned the girls closely about it and they had no idea what I was talking about."

"A fairy what?" asked West. He didn't know what Gardner was talking about either.

"Bower," Gardner explained. "It's a simple woven sheaf that creates a magnetic field out of the sun's rays—a kind of reviving bath for the fairies. They have been seen often before, of course, in the New Forest mainly, but the girls had never heard of them. How can you fake something you're never heard of?" Gardner finished with a look of satisfied glee. Sir Arthur nodded his agreement.

In the conference room, Sir Arthur and Gardner sat on one side of the long table. The chief executive of Kodak, Mr. Binley, the chief technician, West, and two other technicians sat on the other side. Binley opened up the file in front of him.

"Gentlemen," he began, clearing his throat. "Our preliminary findings suggest that the negative plates may indeed be untouched single exposures. However, these findings cannot be taken as conclusive."

"How is that, Mr. Binley?" Sir Arthur asked, calmly.

"Well, the possibility still exists that a clever

operator of great skill might have made them artifi-
cially," Binley said. "Therefore, I must—"

"Clever operator?" Gardner interrupted. "Good
heavens, gentlemen, the girls are eight and twelve
years old. They are the children of ordinary working
men. What cleverness would you afford them?"

Sir Arthur placed a restraining hand on
Gardner's arm.

"I'm sorry," said Binley, closing his file. "I
regret that Kodak must deny your request for a cer-
tificate of authenticity."

West flicked his own file shut, shaking his head
in disbelief.

"You have something to add, sir?" Gardner
asked, turning to West.

"Really, Mr. Gardner," West said in disgust.
"You are asking of Kodak nothing less than to ver-
ify the existence of fairies. Who's next, Father
Christmas?"

"Gentlemen," said Sir Arthur, rising to his
intimidating height, "I accept your decision, but
not your findings. If these photographs are indeed
real, and nothing I have heard this morning
convinces me that they are not, then we are facing
the single most important discovery of our
century—one that must affect every aspect of

our lives, and our beliefs. In this regard, I accept the Kodak Company's unwillingness to bear the burden of proof. However, the photographs speak for themselves. And what is, gentlemen, simply *is*."

Sir Arthur collected his hat and umbrella. "Come, Edward. Duty demands that we act."

"What exactly do you mean by 'act'?" Gardner asked Sir Arthur on their way out of the building.

"We publish," Sir Arthur said decisively. "In next month's issue of *The Strand*."

"Of course," said Gardner. "We publish. But what about the children?"

"Simple. We'll change the names. The innocent must be protected."

"Yes, I see," Gardner replied, not sure that he did. "But won't we be putting their photographs in a national magazine?"

"We most certainly will," Sir Arthur responded.

Gardner was doubtful about the amount of protection the girls would receive once the magazine hit newsstands all over England. But he kept his thoughts to himself.

Almost as soon as *The Strand* rolled off the press, it was snapped up by greedy hands, and the fairies became the talk of the country. In the streets and in the shops, people couldn't get over the amazing discovery. News of the war took a back seat to the story of two little girls and the fairies they'd photographed.

Even the soldiers in the hospitals found the story fascinating. One young man in a wheelchair read the article out loud to his heavily bandaged friend.

"Iris claimed that she and her cousin Alice continually saw fairies and had come to be on familiar and friendly terms with them."

"Well, you'd have to be, wouldn't you?" his friend said seriously. "Otherwise they'd take you away."

"You'll get taken away, all right," said the first young soldier, laughing.

In the *Bradford Argus* newsroom, the editor had his feet up on his desk, reading *The Strand*. John Ferret, the reporter, was sitting at his desk, typing.

"Well, what do you know?" said the editor to Ferret. "They've discovered fairies in Yorkshire."

Ferret looked up from his typing. "Poppycock," he said.

"Not according to Sir Arthur Conan Doyle," replied the editor, pointing at the article.

Ferret grabbed the magazine. "Whereabouts were they taken, can you tell?" he asked, looking closely at the photos.

"I have no idea," replied the editor with a shrug. "Why don't *you* find out?"

Father, Mother, Elsie, and Frances were seated around the kitchen table, each with a copy of *The Strand*. Sir Arthur had sent four copies in the post and they had just arrived. There was a stunned silence until Elsie said, "This is terrible!" The fairies had been betrayed once again.

"Do they get this magazine in France?" Frances wanted to know. She wondered if her father would see the photograph and be pleased that she looked so well.

"*France?*" Father said. "They get the flippin' thing at the North Pole!"

"Arthur Wright, we agreed," Mother said, frowning. "We tried to stop this whole thing once before, and look where that got us. Besides, they've changed all of our names. No one will ever know it's us. Mr. Gardner explained that, remember?"

But Father was not convinced. He knew newspaper people had a way of digging up information. They never quit once they were on the trail of a good story. He was sure there were clues in Sir Arthur Conan Doyle's article that wouldn't be hard for the right kind of reporter to piece together. Before long, there would be someone banging on the door demanding to know more.

Ferret *had* found a clue. He asked an old print worker about the beck in the photograph, and in particular about the waterfall in the photograph's background.

"It could be the Black Hills, up by the reservoir," the man said, shrugging. "There are several becks that come down from there, but only two, as far as I remember, with waterfalls: Mytholme and Cottingley."

"Thank you," replied Ferret, and rushed off.

Ferret jumped onto his motorbike and headed for the first beck. But Mytholme was filthy, overflowing with rubbish and waste from the nearby mill. It didn't look in the least like the magical place in the photograph. There wasn't a fairy on earth who would live in Mytholme!

When he reached Cottingley, Ferret knew

exactly where to go: to the only school in the village. He would find out where those two girls lived and blow Sir Arthur Conan Doyle's story right out of the water!

Chapter Ten

Mrs. Thornton recognized the fairy in the newspaper article. It looked just like the fairies one of her students, Elsie, was always drawing! Ferret looked at a drawing tacked on the wall and smiled when he saw the name written at the bottom: ELSIE WRIGHT, AGE 12 YEARS. Here was his second clue!

When Ferret banged on the front door of the Wright home, Father answered.

"Mr. Wright?" Ferret asked.

"Yes," Father said with a sinking feeling.

"Mr. Arthur Wright?" Ferret pressed, just to make sure.

Father frowned. "Who wants to know?" he asked.

The reporter held up his notepad. "John Ferret, *Bradford Argus*..."

Father slammed the door in Ferret's face. Inside the house, he stood with his back to the door and his eyes closed. He knew this was only the beginning.

"It's no use slamming the door, Mr. Wright, I won't go until I've got my story."

In answer, Father turned off all the lights in the house.

That night, the wind howled angrily around the eaves of the house, making the attic room seem an unfriendly, spooky place. Perhaps the fairies had told the wind to scold the girls for breaking their promise. Elsie and Frances were wide awake, with their covers pulled up high.

"What are we going to do?" Frances whispered nervously. "We promised we'd never tell."

"They'll never come out now," Elsie agreed. "We'll never see them again."

"Perhaps we could give them something," suggested Frances.

"Like what?" Elsie said. She was sure there was no gift special enough.

"Something to let them know that we're sorry."

Elsie thought for a moment. "Like cake?"

But Frances didn't think that would be special enough. She gazed round the room, looking for the perfect gift. Finally, she spied it in the corner.

"The doll house!" she cried, jumping out of bed.

"We can't," said Elsie, shocked. "It was Joseph's."

"So?"

"Mum would kill me," Elsie said.

"Who did he make it for, then?" reasoned Frances.

"The fairies," Elsie admitted.

At that, the windows rattled all the louder and a chill ran down Elsie's spine.

"Well, then?" pressed Frances.

"But it isn't finished," said Elsie, hoping to change her cousin's mind.

"We can finish it," said Frances, and it was settled.

The girls worked all night, pulling laces from their shoes, taking feathers from their pillows, using shoeboxes and biscuit tins and anything else they could find. They giggled and whispered and squirted glue on each other. By dawn they were worn out, but the house was finished.

*   *   *

The early morning sky was gray and dreary and the morning mist was cool. Tired but happy, the girls lugged the house to the beck, groaning under the weight they carried between them. They set the doll house in a small clearing. Elsie looked around at the gloomy forest.

"Queen Mab?" she called tentatively.

Silence was the only response.

"Prince Malekin!" Frances shouted. "Come see what we've brought you. It's a palace!"

The girls separated, searching for fairies. As she walked through the woods, Elsie called out names.

"Shellycoat, where are you? Tib, we have cake. Peerifool... Oh, it's no use, they won't come," Elsie fretted. "They're here, but they won't come out."

Elsie sat down, discouraged, while in another part of the woods Frances searched on. "Gull, you can come out now," she called. "Nanny Buttoncap, Princess Florella..."

The shadows of the trees grew shorter as the sun drank in more of the morning sky. Frances was slowly becoming as frustrated as Elsie. Suddenly, she heard the crunch of leaves directly behind her. She spun around, frightened.

"Elsie? Is that you?"

In a panic, Frances broke into a run. There was someone—or something—behind her, and it didn't sound like a fairy! Frances tried not to trip on the stones under her feet. Suddenly, a man jumped out in front of her!

"W-who're you?" asked Frances, frightened.

"Someone in search of the truth," said the man. It was Ferret, the reporter.

"The t-truth?" Frances stammered.

"I'm not in the mood for baby games," said Ferret. "Sir Arthur Conan Doyle put you up to all this, didn't he?"

"W-who?" replied Frances, stalling for time.

"Sir Arthur Conan Doyle, that's who."

"No, he did not," Frances said firmly.

She was slowly moving away, planning to make a run for it. But before she could, Ferret grabbed her by the shoulder.

"Don't lie to me," he said, shaking her roughly.

Just then, Elsie came running up.

"Leave her alone!" she cried, standing in front of Frances. "If you don't go away right now," she continued, "the fairies are going to come out and box your ears!"

Ferret smirked but glanced around nervously anyway. All was quiet in the glade. "Sure they are," he scoffed.

Suddenly, there was the sound of leaves crunching once again. Ferret frowned, even more nervous now. "You don't fool me," he said, uncertain.

Elsie caught a glimpse of a figure dressed in black moving in the trees behind Ferret. Ferret leaned down ominously and looked Elsie in the eye.

"The truth now," he said.

Suddenly, a hand grabbed Ferret by the shoulder. Slowly, he turned—and looked into the face of a monster! He screamed in terror and ran off. Elsie stepped back, horrified by the man with half a face. But Frances ran forward and threw her arms around him. "The corporal!" she shouted joyfully. It was her friend from the train!

The corporal hugged Frances, gently stroking her hair, and smiled at Elsie. The smile made his face warm and friendly, and Elsie was no longer afraid. Then, sitting down beside the doll house, the corporal told the girls how he'd found them.

"Forgive me if I startled you," he said. "I saw the photographs in *The Strand* and I recognized Frances right away. I don't want to disturb the fairies. I just need to know....are they real?"

The corporal seemed to be asking the girls to give him back all the hope he'd lost in the war. It was a huge request, but Elsie didn't want to be the one to cause the corporal any more pain. She nodded yes when Frances looked at her questioningly.

The corporal smiled and drew Elsie into a hug. "I knew it," he said happily.

Elsie gazed out into the woods, wondering at how easy it was to break a promise—even when you had no intention of doing so.

Houdini had also read *The Strand* article. He decided to invite Sir Arthur to visit him at the theater. He had something to show the famous author. In his darkroom, Houdini had made a print that showed him sitting across from the ghost of Abraham Lincoln.

"Double exposure," Sir Arthur said, looking at the photo. "It was the first thing Snelling looked for. And Kodak spent three days trying to find evidence of it and found nothing."

"They didn't look hard enough," Houdini said. "This is how I earn my living, creating pictures in the dark. Pictures for people to believe in. Look at this."

Houdini took Sir Arthur into another room and showed him the arrangement of steps and mirrors that made it look as if his head was floating in midair above his body. "People want to believe in the impossible because they want the impossible to enter their lives," he said.

Sir Arthur did not reply.

"So they come to watch me, the great Houdini, locked in the trunk, chained in the tank, trussed up in the air like a Thanksgiving turkey," the illusionist went on. "They come to watch me die. That's why I wait until the very last moment to escape. I wait until they begin to think I must have failed. Then I wait some more, until they're sure of it—sure that I've crossed the line, passed over. Then the impossible happens in front of their eyes and I come back. I am alive! I am their fairy story once a night and twice on matinee days."

Houdini told Sir Arthur he didn't lie to his audience. He just didn't tell them the whole truth. They knew the tricks he performed were games, the same way they knew that Sherlock Holmes didn't exist.

"There's no deception, no promise of messages, no supernatural beings," Houdini said. "I despise false mediums who claim to be able to contact the dead. I expose their lies whenever I can."

Sir Arthur quoted the inscription he had seen at the bottom of one of Houdini's pictures of his mother. "You're looking for a real medium," he said. "That's why you expose the false ones."

"There isn't a real one," Houdini said firmly. "I've made it my business to know."

"You know everything, but you believe nothing," Sir Arthur told him. "And you'll never find what you're looking for until you do."

In Cottingley Glen that night, the doll house glowed faintly. Slowly, the fairies came out of hiding. They floated down from tree branches and came out from under toadstools. Lob went inside the doll house and stuck his head out of a window. Mr. Bandylegs, the gnome, came out of the door and walked along the bridge that led to the ground. The fairies Morgana and Prince Malekin flew down to get a closer look. It was a magical night in Cottingley Glen. It was the night the fairies accepted Joseph's gift.

Chapter Eleven

Ferret's fright in the woods at Cottingley didn't stop him from writing his story. The night the fairies moved into the doll house, Ferret worked late. When the first paper came off the press the next morning, he smiled in satisfaction at the headline: LOCAL GIRLS CLAIM FAIRIES AT BOTTOM OF GARDEN.

Once the paper hit the stands, there was an instant fairy frenzy. People everywhere started for Cottingley, traveling by whatever means they could: by foot, by bike, by wagon or automobile. They simply had to see the fairies—or better yet, try and capture one!

Cottingley Beck was peaceful in the mist of the early morning. The animals in the glade knew nothing of the outside world. A fox slipped down the slope to take a drink from the stream. A rabbit watched from under a hollow log. Suddenly, the fox looked up from drinking. It had heard an unusual sound. The rabbit was also on the alert. Suddenly, the morning's peace was shattered by a throng of noisy people cresting the hill and descending into the glen.

The fox and the rabbit ran for cover. A huge flock of small birds scattered into the sky, wheeling in silence before flying off. A bus full of fairy-seekers stampeded into the glen, producing a cloud of smoke and dust. The beck was crawling with people looking for fairies.

But the fairies were leaving. A sad, slow procession of elves, some riding tiny white horses, most walking, crossed the road leading away from the beck. The fairies were abandoning Cottingley Glen!

At school, Elsie and Frances were unaware that their magical world was in danger. They were busy copying the drawing of a bee that Mrs. Thornton had put on the board. Suddenly, Father appeared in the doorway.

"Excuse me, Mrs. Thornton," he said urgently. "I must take the girls home. Elsie! Frances!"

Father hustled them out of the classroom and into the van.

"In you get," he said, quickly slamming the door.

"Dad, what's going on?" Elsie asked, frightened. "Is it Mum?"

Father didn't answer. He started up the van and tore off for home. At the Wright house, there was already a crowd of people gathered at the door. Even Albert the postman wanted to know if the story was true.

"So, what's this all about, Arthur?" he asked.

"It's all rubbish, Albert," Father said. "It's all rubbish. Go home, please. All of you!" He herded the girls to the front door.

"Inside, you two. *Now!*" he said. Elsie and Frances ran into the house.

Ferret stuck his head through the door. "Girls! I'd like to ask you a few questions!" he called after them.

Father blocked his way. "Get back, you!" he said.

But Ferret wouldn't give up so easily. "Did Sir Arthur put you up to it?" he called out to Elsie and Frances.

Father gave Ferret a shove.

"Stay out of my house," he said, and slammed the door shut.

Mother stood by the window, alarmed. This wasn't supposed to happen. They were all supposed to be protected from this kind of craziness.

"Keep the girls here," Father said. "I'm going to find Constable Leigh."

From the attic window, Elsie and Frances saw the hordes of people crashing into the beck. They looked on in horror, imagining how awful it must be for their friends, the fairies. What would happen to them? Would they be able to escape? Surely now they would *never* return to live in the beck. The magic was being trampled underfoot by the uncaring mob!

"They'll never come back now, will they?" Frances said, thinking of the doll house.

"Did you see the way my dad looked at me?" Elsie asked. She choked back tears. "He's never looked at me like that before."

As horrible as losing the fairies was, the thought of losing her father's love was even more terrible. Elsie could not even bear to think of it.

Meanwhile, people kept searching for the fairies. Couples, families, kids from school, soldiers from the war, the very young and the very old were turning over every leaf and stone to find even just *one* fairy.

"Here, fairies, good little fairies!" called an elderly woman.

A man dressed in white robes marched through the glade, beating a drum. A soldier stepped on Elsie's twig dining set, crushing it into pieces. A young boy called out, "I caught one! Come see. Is *this* a fairy?" A crowd gathered round, but it was only a toad that hopped out of the boy's open hands.

While all this chaos was happening, Ferret leaned against a nearby tree, smiling wickedly and scribbling notes onto his notepad.

Suddenly, there were two loud gunshots! Everyone froze. It was Mr. Briggs with his game-keepers and his big dogs.

"Everybody here is trespassing on my land!" he shouted. "If you are still here in five minutes, I'll set my dogs on the lot of you!"

Ferret stumbled up the slope toward Briggs. He had a question to ask.

"Excuse me, sir," he said. "Do you believe there are fairies at the bottom of your garden?"

"Do I look as though I believe in fairies?" Briggs blustered.

"Well, if they *do* exist," Ferret pressed, "are you considering charging them rent, sir?"

Cottingley Beck was a mess of sandwich papers, leftover food scraps, and newspapers blowing in the breeze. Elsie and Frances could hardly bear to look at the scene.

"They're gone," Frances whispered, almost in tears. "They've left us."

"It's my fault," Elsie said.

"*I* thought of the camera," said Frances.

"No, you didn't," Elsie said, frowning.

"I certainly did," replied Frances, angrily.

"Did not," said Elsie, giving her cousin a push.

"Did!" said Frances, pushing back.

"Didn't!"

Frances lunged toward Elsie and the two girls fell to the ground. They rolled down the slope, kicking and fighting. Suddenly, a twig snapped and the two girls froze in fright. Frances took Elsie's hand. Slowly and cautiously, a young deer came into the clearing. It saw the girls from across the stream but bent its head just the same to take a drink.

"Do you think perhaps they're still here?" asked Frances, hopefully.

"Shh! No, I don't," Elsie replied. "We've

driven them away. All those people with their dirty cars and their great big boots. The fairies will never come back."

Deep down, Elsie was glad of it. Perhaps it was just as well that the fairies no longer lived in the beck, for they would always be in danger from those who did not understand them.

Chapter Twelve

Frances knew the magic was over. And it was all because of a few silly photographs. The next morning, she took down all the photos of her family that she'd clipped around the mirror and threw them into a drawer. She didn't want to see them anymore.

"Frances, what are you doing?" asked Elsie. It seemed as though her cousin was being overly harsh and destructive. "Please don't do that."

"I'm tired of photographs," Frances said.

Then she threw herself facedown on the bed.

When the postman's bell sounded, Frances didn't hear it. Ever since the day she'd arrived at the Wrights', she'd run out every morning to see if the package from France had been delivered. Today,

Frances didn't seem to care. But Elsie ran to the window.

"Frances," she reminded her cousin.

"Frances! Frances Griffiths!" Albert called out from the front garden.

Frances jumped up and bolted for the trapdoor, nearly knocking the startled postman down as she threw open the door and grabbed the package.

"Hope it's what you've been expecting," Albert said. He seemed worried that it might be bad news.

But it was the perfume from France! The package looked like as if it had traveled around the world twice. Inside was a tiny Limoges porcelain bottle.

"Who knows how long it's been in the post," said Father, looking at all the stamps and stickers on the package. He and Mother had the same thought, but they kept it to themselves.

Upstairs, the perfume box lay open on Frances's bedside table. The note stuck inside it read: I ALWAYS KEEP MY PROMISES. LOVE, DADDY.

"It's a good thing it didn't break," Elsie said, touching the delicate bottle. Like her parents, she, too, feared that Frances's father might be dead, but she didn't want to say the words out loud.

Frances dabbed a touch of perfume on her wrist and then put some behind Elsie's ears. "How does it smell?" she asked.

"Très jolie," Elsie responded in her best French accent.

"Jolly?" asked Frances, confused.

"No," Elsie said, smiling. "It means pretty. Very pretty."

The girls laughed together. They were friends once more, their fight at the beck forgotten.

"We weren't so bad, really," said Frances, thinking of the fairies again. "The photographs made people happy."

"I'm just glad it's over," Elsie said.

It was a golden afternoon at the beck. Elsie was sitting alone on the fallen log bridge, swinging her legs and watching leaves float past her in the stream. Suddenly, a voice broke into her daydream.

"It *is* beautiful here, isn't it?" said Father. He drank in the beauty of the trees for a moment and listened to the gentle flow of the beck. "I can see why you children love it so," he said finally, sitting down beside Elsie. As he did, he noticed splatters of paint on the log.

"Joseph?" he asked.

Elsie nodded. Then she asked the question that had been on her mind for months.

"Dad, why did you make him stop?"

Father sighed. "Joseph was nearly eleven when he died," he answered. "He would have started half-time work at the mill in another year. His childhood was over, but he wouldn't let go of it. It was his time to grow up. Yours is coming, too, you know."

Suddenly, from a distance, Elsie's name rang through the trees.

"Elsie!"

She and Father looked up to see Mother and Frances racing down the slope. Mother was waving a piece of paper over her head.

"Arthur! London!" she called out excitedly.

Mother and Frances splashed into the stream, stopping for an instant to catch their breath.

"What are you talking about?" Father asked.

"London! We're going to London!" replied Mother.

"Sir Arthur invited us!" Frances added.

"Why?" Elsie asked.

"Sir Arthur Conan Doyle has written a book about the fairies," Mother said, handing the telegram to Father. "He wants us there for the publication."

Elsie covered her face with her hands. In an instant, the golden afternoon was gone. There would never be an escape from those photographs!

At the Bradford station, a crowd gathered around the Wright family. There were reporters asking questions and photographers taking pictures. The girls were celebrities, whether they liked it or not.

"Are you going to be looking for fairies in Kensington Gardens, then, girls?" asked one photographer.

Several flashes went off at once as more photos were taken. This was a big adventure for Elsie and Frances.

As Father directed his family toward their train, he heard his name being called above the clamor. Mr. Briggs also had an invitation to Sir Arthur's book party. When he saw that Father and his family were the reason for all the hubbub, he shouted:

"Arthur! What in heaven's name is going on?"

"The family is making a brief trip to London," Father said.

"But what are you doing in...?" Briggs began.

"Sir Arthur Conan Doyle insisted that they travel first class," Father replied, pleased to see the look of surprise on his employer's face.

"Sir Arthur?" said Briggs.

"Excuse me," Father said. "I've got to get every-one settled."

Father made sure that the luggage was safely stowed and tipped the porter. Elsie and Frances found seats by the window while Mother said good-bye to Father.

"Are you sure you won't come?" she asked one last time.

"What would happen if one of those journalists asked me what I thought?" Father said. "I'd have to tell them, wouldn't I? Besides, I've got the chess match to play at the pub and the manor to take care of with Mr. Briggs away. So don't worry about me. You and the girls enjoy yourselves."

The train's whistle blew. Mother grabbed Father for one final hug. "Good luck in the tournament," she said.

The guard waved the green flag and the great engine let out a huge cloud of steam as the train began to move out of the station. Father stood on the platform and waved good-bye.

At the *Bradford Argus*, the editor dropped a copy of next morning's edition on Ferret's desk.

"I see your girls are to be the toast of London,"

he said. "Says here the fairies are bringing hope back to the Empire."

Ferret stopped his work to look at the headline. "Fakes—the whole nasty lot of them!" he said angrily.

"Well, there's no one who's proved that," said the editor meaningfully.

Just then Ferret had a brilliant idea. "The family's in London, you say?" he asked with a sly smile. "Hmm…"

In London, the girls were treated to double-decker bus rides and theater tickets. Photographers followed them everywhere they went. Frances began to enjoy having her picture taken, and posed prettily for each new shot. Even Mother was finding the adventure exciting. Only Elsie found each day more difficult than the one before.

One day, they were given a guided tour of the children's ward at St. Thomas Hospital. There were children in wheelchairs, on crutches, and confined to bed. As the girls walked through the ward, children reached out to touch them. A boy named Michael, sick with a fever, called out to Frances.

"Miss?" he asked. "Could you please ask your fairies to come and help me get better?"

"I'll try," said Frances.

The London trip had made Frances more of a believer than ever. She was certain that the fairies could heal the boy if she asked them. But Elsie knew it wasn't true. She didn't think it was right for Frances to give Michael false hope. When Frances moved on with the photographers, Elsie went over to his bed.

"Fairies can't help you get well," she said gently. She immediately felt unkind as she said it, for a look of despair came across Michael's face. "You have to ask your guardian angel for that," she added.

"I have an angel?" asked Michael hopefully.

"Of course," replied Elsie. "We all do. They help us get through the bad times."

Michael beamed. Elsie turned to find Mother standing behind her.

"That was nice," Mother said. "I'm so proud of you. Then she whispered, looking deep into her daughter's eyes, "Thank you."

"For what?" asked Elsie, in surprise.

Mother put her arm around her daughter as they walked out of the ward.

"For the photographs."

Elsie's step faltered briefly.

* * *

At Sir Arthur's book party, Houdini excused himself and went into the study, where he sat down at the desk. Suddenly, he looked over his shoulder, sensing someone else in the room. Elsie was watching him from the shadows.

"Hiding?" Houdini asked.

"No. I mean, well, yes," Elsie said.

"Come here, Elsie," said Houdini. "Do you like fruit?"

She nodded. "Yes."

"Apples or pears?"

"Pears," said Elsie.

She was astounded when Houdini produced a pear, a napkin, a knife, and a plate—all out of thin air!

"Can you manage, or would you like a table?" he asked, with a sly smile.

Elsie couldn't imagine how even the great Houdini would pull a table out of thin air.

"No, thank you," she said quickly. "Mr. Houdini, do you mind if I ask you a question?"

"Go ahead," Houdini replied.

"Do you ever tell anyone how you do things?" asked Elsie. "You know, just to see the look on their faces?"

"Never," replied Houdini. "Ever. And I never will, not even when I'm dead. And shall I tell you something important? No one ever really wants to know when you *do* tell them. Now can I ask *you* a question?"

"Yes," said Elsie hesitantly.

"Will you come and see my show?"

Elsie gave him a big smile.

Of course she would! This would be the best part of the trip—seeing the great Houdini perform his incredible feats of magic.

Chapter Thirteen

Elsie, Frances, and Mother were guests of honor at the Hippodrome Theatre. Houdini was on stage, swallowing a long piece of thread and a handful of needles. Elsie and Frances squirmed in their seats at the thought of the needles sticking in his throat.

Houdini swallowed the last needle. Then, very slowly, he began tugging a line out of his mouth. One by one, the needles appeared, all neatly threaded! Houdini pulled the last needle out of his mouth and gave a quick bow. Elsie and Frances led the enthusiastic applause.

Then Houdini clapped his hands twice and five stage assistants wheeled out his famous Chinese Water Torture Tank.

*　　*　　*

The pub in Cottingley Village had a poster in the window: THE YORKSHIRE CHESS CHALLENGE! MR. SIDNEY CHALKER CHALLENGES ALL COMERS TO A TEST OF SKILL.

Father sat quietly while Chalker's manager addressed the crowd.

"Gentlemen, we will match penny for penny any purse you care to raise. In fairness, I must warn you that Mr. Chalker here is the undisputed champion of this country. He is respected among the chess players in every major town within a hundred miles of here!"

Chalker was a large man with a serious expression and very big hands. He wasn't able to speak, but his grunts showed that he was pleased at his manager's words. A red-faced man suddenly stepped out of the crowd and put a coin on the table in front of Chalker.

"My money's on Arthur Wright of Cottingley!"

There was a murmur of approval among the customers. Suddenly, men began stepping up from every direction to place their money on the table in favor of Father.

Outside the Wright house, Ferret was looking for an open window. Earlier that evening, he had gone down to the beck and destroyed the fairy doll house, kicking it angrily. He was sick to death of this whole hoax. One way or another, he was determined to find out the truth!

Ferret had already tried the back door and found it locked. But the first window he tried was unlocked. He opened it, and looking around to make sure no one saw him, quickly climbed in.

In the kitchen, Ferret shone his lantern into every corner of the room but found nothing.

Houdini's Chinese Water Torture Tank was a tall glass tank filled with water. The stage assistants wrapped Houdini in thick chains with locks on each chain. The chains were fastened tightly and the locks were checked and double-checked. Then Houdini's legs were fitted into a wooden clamp and locked. He was hoisted upside down into the air, directly above the tank, and slowly lowered into the water.

Once Houdini was completely submerged, the top of the tank was bolted into place. The escape artist was now tightly bound in chains, underwater, with no escape! Elsie and Frances sat on the edge of their seats, watching Houdini's eyes bulge as he began the struggle to free himself. Then a curtain was slowly lowered in front of the tank, and the audience could no longer see the struggle.

In the early stages of the chess game at Cottingley Pub, Father had lost one of his major pieces, a bishop. Chalker sat grinning happily at him across the board. The crowd grumbled its disappointment. Perhaps Arthur Wright hadn't been the man to back, after all.

Chalker grunted whenever it was Father's turn to make a move. He grunted now, and Father, after much concentration, moved a pawn forward. This piece was swiftly captured by Chalker. The crowd burst into another groan.

Father tried to remain calm. It wasn't wise to give away one's nervousness by showing emotion. For his next turn, Father moved a pawn and took one of Chalker's knights. There was a loud cheer from the crowd. Father had scored!

At the Wright house, Ferret was moving quietly and carefully around the attic bedroom, being careful to keep the lantern away from the window. But there was nothing of interest in the girls' room.

Ferret walked down the trapdoor steps and saw a door he'd overlooked—Joseph's room! He opened the door and immediately knew that this room held the secret. He placed the lantern on the desk and began opening the drawers. Within moments, he had found Joseph's folder. He pulled it out and grinned when he saw the drawings. He was sure he had found the secret behind the fairy photographs!

Houdini was struggling with every ounce of his strength. Before being put into the tank, he had asked the audience to hold their breath when one of the stage assistants gave the signal. The moment Houdini went underwater, the assistant had done so—and everyone had run out of air long ago!

Elsie was sure her face had turned purple by now. She had held her breath for as long as she could before giving up and gasping for air. Now she waited anxiously. What if this time the escape was too much for Houdini? What if this time her friend drowned?

Mother leaned down and whispered, "Don't worry, Elsie. It's only a trick. Like the circus."

Ferret placed the cutout fairy drawings he'd found in Joseph's folder out on the desk. Then he pulled out the clipping from the newspaper. The fairies in the photograph looked just like the ones in the drawings! Ferret smiled in satisfaction. He had done a good night's work!

Just then, he noticed that the wind was starting to howl much louder. The flame in his lantern was flickering. Suddenly, the bedroom window blew open and the drawings quickly scattered. Ferret tried to gather them up, but the fairy drawings danced like real fairies in the air around him. Then, just as suddenly as it started, the wind stopped and all was silent again. The scattered papers fell gently to the floor.

Behind the curtain at the Hippodrome, Houdini had carefully removed a small piece of wire from his mouth. Even though he'd been searched by members of the audience, he had still been able to keep the wire hidden secret.

Quickly, the illusionist started to pick the locks and undo the chains. In a matter of seconds, he was free! Then he picked the lock that bolted the lid shut. The audience heard the lock click open. As the curtain was raised, Houdini burst out of the tank, gasping for air.

The audience couldn't believe their eyes. Everyone in the theater went crazy with applause.

*   *   *

At Cottingley Pub, there was excitement in the air as the chess match neared the end. Each player had only five pieces left, and it was Chalker's move. He hesitated, then made up his mind to move a knight. Father quickly made his move in response and cornered Chalker's king.

"Checkmate!" he said quietly.

The crowd burst into applause. Chalker's manager started angrily toward the table, but the crowd held him back. Chalker just stared at the chessboard. There was dead silence in the room. Then the supposedly mute Chalker looked up at Father and muttered a few impolite words. The room burst into laughter and cheers as Father was congratulated. He was the winner of the big tournament!

The door to Joseph's room was locked, and Ferret was trapped! The dancing papers had spooked him, and now, in the half-light, he could see the pale figure of a boy sitting at the desk, concentrating on his drawing. The boy got up and very slowly walked toward Ferret, who had backed up against the door. The boy didn't seem to see Ferret. *He walked straight through him!* Ferret took one look at the open window and jumped out.

* * *

After the show, Houdini was surrounded by reporters. One asked him what he thought of the fairies in the photographs. Did he think they were real?

"I have spent my life making the impossible true. Why would I find it hard to accept it in others?" Houdini replied.

"Because you have always refused to tolerate lies and trickery," came the reporter's response.

"Sir, I have fought those who would make money out of the grief and pain of others," Houdini said. "I stand against the exploitation of suffering mothers whose dead children are paraded before their grieving eyes. I see none of that here. I see only joy." He leaned down to hug Elsie and Frances.

The reporter asked Houdini one last question. "Any chance you'd tell us how you escaped from the tank?"

"Masters of illusion never reveal their secrets," Houdini said, winking at Elsie. "Thank you, gentlemen."

As Father headed home from Cottingley Pub, he saw that pesky reporter weaving down the street on his motorbike. Ferret looked as if he'd fallen into a coal-bin. He made a sudden swerve on his bike and crashed into a mailbox. Father watched in amazement as the reporter got up and hobbled off into the darkness.

Chapter Fourteen

In the Royal Suite in a London hotel, Elsie lay in a huge canopy bed, with the covers pulled up to her chin and a thermometer stuck in her mouth. Mother read her temperature.

"You're fine," she pronounced. "Just very, very tired."

Frances sighed. She knew her cousin wasn't enjoying the London trip.

"We don't deserve any of this," Elsie told her, looking around at the luxurious room.

"Someone thinks we do," said Frances. She was very happy being treated like royalty.

"We're not heroes, Frances," Elsie said. "I just

want to go home. I just want everything to be the way it was before."

When the London trip was finally over, life in Cottingley Village began to return to normal. One morning, Elsie found Mother in Joseph's room, packing his things into a box. She stopped outside the door.

"Mum? What are you doing?" she asked.

"I don't think Joseph would mind it terribly if you moved in here," Mother said, smiling.

"Really?"

"Really," Mother said, giving Elsie a big hug.

From the hallway, hidden in shadow, Frances watched sadly. That night, she asked Elsie if she was going to have to live in Cottingley forever. Elsie assured her cousin it wouldn't be so, but even as she said it, she couldn't be sure.

"I know what it means when they say my dad is *missing*," Frances said quietly.

"It just means they don't know where he is," replied Elsie gently.

Frances changed the subject. "What does it feel like when you grow up?" she asked.

"I don't know," Elsie said. "I think it feels different for everybody."

"Do you want to grow up?" Frances asked.

Elsie thought for a moment. "Yes. I think I do."

"Even if it means never seeing the fairies again?" Frances persisted.

"It doesn't matter, not seeing them again," said Elsie. "We'll never forget, like everybody else who grows up. Because we have the photographs. That's why they're so important. Whenever we start to forget or pretend we never knew, we can look at them and we'll remember."

"I think I know how it is to be grown up," said Frances, thoughtfully. "It's when you can feel...how someone feels...who isn't you."

Late that night, a truck with SUNLIGHT SOAP written across the side barreled across the moors toward Cottingley Village. Suddenly, a flash of silver moonlight glinted on the beck and a fish leaped out of the water. The surface closed and became still again. Another light skated on the stream. It was Queen Mab, skimming on her tiny feet. She sprang up and turned somersaults in the air, flying toward Elsie's house.

All sorts of other fairies slid and twisted across the water, following their queen. The fairies flew down the Wrights' chimney and spilled into the house. Hob and Lob pulled open the window and more fairies drifted into the house and up the stairs to the girls' room.

The truck rumbled on across the moors, moving closer and closer to the Wright house. The headlights scanned the road ahead as the truck bounced in a rut and rounded a corner.

In the quiet of the attic room, the fairies swarmed like brilliant bees. Suddenly, Elsie opened her eyes and looked around. There were fairies everywhere—standing on the backs of chairs and on top of the wardrobe and sitting in the rafters!

Slowly, Elsie rose from her bed while Frances slept on. She stood before Queen Mab and bowed low. Then she offered her finger to the beautiful fairy, who took it and held it, flying up as Elsie raised her into the air. Elsie walked across the room and leaned over Frances with Queen Mab sitting on her shoulder.

"Frances!" she whispered. "Frances!"

Frances sat up quickly and the fairies scattered. She stared straight ahead, as though she were looking through the roof into the sky. She didn't see even one of the creatures of the air that filled the room.

"Listen," she said earnestly. She'd heard an engine outside the window.

The Sunlight truck had stopped outside the

Wright house. Feet crunched on the ground and a door slammed. Frances ran to the window. The truck was gone, but someone was walking up to the door! Frances raced downstairs and frantically pulled open the door. There, in the doorway, stood her beloved father, home from the war.

"Daddy!" Frances shouted.

Mother and Father had awakened and were standing in the doorway of their bedroom when they both saw Lob fly by. They exchanged glances in amazement, but said nothing.

Elsie gazed up into the rafters. All of the fairies were standing there, looking down at her.

"Thank you," she said, softly.

Frances's father picked up his daughter and hugged her.

"That perfume smells good," he said.

"But I'm not wearing any," Frances said.

"I know," said her father, and closed the door.

Epilogue

On June 22, 1922, in Atlantic City, New Jersey, Sir Arthur Conan Doyle was convinced that he had made successful contact with Houdini's dead mother. Houdini was present at the time, but the illusionist did not believe it to be true.

Shortly before her death in 1988, Elsie Wright admitted that four of the five photographs she'd taken of the fairies had been created using paper cutouts stuck on hatpins. But she would not admit that the fifth photograph was also fake, and it remains a mystery to this day.

*   *   *

For all their lives, both Frances and Elsie continued to claim that they had definitely seen fairies in Cottingley Glen.